Karen McC[...] is the best-sellin[...] of the *Indie Kidd* series, as well as other fiction for children and teenagers. She used to write for magazines *J17* and *Sugar*. Karen lives in London with her husband, small daughter and two fat cats.

♡ ♡ ♡

Lydia Monks won the Smarties Prize for *I Wish I Were a Dog*. She has illustrated many poetry, novelty and picture books for children, including the *Girl Zone* series for Walker. Lydia lives in Sheffield with her husband and daughter.

For Dylan Hood (Indie's got
her Dylan but this one's mine!)
KMcC

This is a work of fiction. Names, characters, places and incidents are
either the product of the author's imagination or, if real, are used fictitiously.

First published 2005 by Walker Books Ltd
87 Vauxhall Walk, London SE11 5HJ

This edition published 2007

2 4 6 8 10 9 7 5 3 1

Text © 2005 Karen McCombie
Illustrations © 2005 Lydia Monks

The right of Karen McCombie and Lydia Monks to be identified as author
and illustrator respectively of this work has been asserted by them in accordance
with the Copyright, Designs and Patents Act 1988

This book has been typeset in Granjon

Printed and bound in Great Britain by
Creative Print and Design (Wales), Ebbw Vale

British Library Cataloguing in Publication Data:
a catalogue record for this book is available from the British Library

ISBN 978-1-4063-0717-7

www.walkerbooks.co.uk

How to be Good (ish)

KAREN McCOMBIE

LYDIA MONKS

WALKER BOOKS
AND SUBSIDIARIES
LONDON · BOSTON · SYDNEY · AUCKLAND

Caitlin

Fee & Soph

D.I.B

Dad

Fiona

Dylan

Miss Levy

Happy birthday to ME!

I was named after a DOG.

For three years, my dad didn't know that.

"India?" he'd said, just after I was born, when my mum suggested it. "India Kidd… We could call her 'Indie' for short. Yeah, I *like* it!"

When Dad was trying my name out for size, he was thinking of spice and heat and beautiful scenery. Mum decided it was best

to let him think she'd been inspired by a very large country, and not the small brown dog with a flea allergy who'd come into the animal shelter where she worked.

India got a new home after only a few days, even though she looked a bit odd

India the dog

(she was a POMERANIAN, which is a kind of dog that's supposed to be as hairy as a sheep, but she'd scratched off her fur with all that itching).

Mum said her lovely temperament and appealing eyes were the reason why India got a new owner so soon. But I reckon someone just thought it would be really cool to have a small bald dog…

Anyway, three years later, when Mum accidentally let the truth about my name slip out, Dad wasn't very pleased. That was around the time they were splitting up, so neither of them was in a very good mood, I don't suppose. But I was little back then, so I don't remember any of that. And I don't really remember a time when Dad wasn't living with my step-mum Fiona and her son Dylan.

I live with Mum, our lodger Caitlin, and all our pets: Kenneth and George (both dogs), Smudge (a cat that looks like a cushion), One, Two, Three, Four and Five (our goldfish) and Brian (a very shy angelfish).

Me and Mum are totally and completely nuts about animals, but not just at home. Mum is the assistant manager of the Paws For Thought Animal Rescue Centre. Mum is so good at looking after sick, hurt or abandoned animals that she sometimes forgets about less important stuff, like people and sleeping and birthdays, for example.

I only mention birthdays because (oops!) Mum forgot my tenth birthday. I didn't blame her, really – I just blamed those baby hedgehogs...

Only joking; I didn't *really* blame the baby hedgehogs (how could you blame something so small, helpless and cute?). And I didn't mind *too* much that Mum had forgotten my birthday just this once; after all, I knew she had other things on her mind, like small, helpless and cute baby hedgehogs, for example.

 The night before, she'd had to get up out of bed and hand-feed them about a zillion times (I'd helped and took a turn at 6 a.m.).

When I came downstairs on the morning of my birthday, my very pretty but very tired-looking Mum was already rushing towards the front door, on her way to work. In fact, she was *so* tired that she nearly forgot something, and I don't just mean my birthday.

"Mum!" I called, holding a small plastic box out to her.

And no – it wasn't her packed lunch; the box was full of snoozly mini-hedgehogs, all curled up in a prickly mound. (OK, so I might not know how to pay bills or assistant-manage a whole animal rescue centre, but there *are* times when I think I'm more grown-up than my ditzy mother…)

"Thanks, Indie!" Mum grinned at me, tucking a tangle of messy blonde hair behind her ear. "You're such a good girl. What would I do without you?"

I felt myself blushing. I can't help it; even if there are times when I feel all grown-up, I still come over all dopey and shy when people give me compliments. (Isn't it funny how you can feel brave one minute and weedy the next?)

Mum gave me a quick kiss on the cheek, took the box of hedgehogs and hurried so fast towards the door that I thought she might trip over George (our greyhound), or the didgeridoo (our lodger Caitlin's), or the BIG pile of post (birthday cards from Dad, and both my grans and everyone).

But somehow Mum managed not to trip, or spill any hedgehogs, and left the house without noticing the telltale birthday cards or the fact that her jumper was on inside-out and back-to-front.

After waving Mum and the hedgehogs off to work, I wandered into the kitchen with my bundle of post and spotted a white envelope on the table, with

KID!

scrawled on it in Caitlin's handwriting.

(Caitlin always calls me 'kid'. I don't mind – mainly 'cause I'm glad it's not my real name; Kid Kidd would be too weird, wouldn't it?)

Inside the envelope was a torn-out bit of paper that read,

Happy Birthday, KID!
IOU a pizza when
I get paid!

Well, it was the thought that counted. Still, I couldn't wait to get to school to see my best friends Soph and Fee. I knew they'd make a real birthday fuss of me, same as I did when it was *their* birthdays…

"SORRYSORRYHAPPY BIRTHDAYBABES!"

I suddenly heard my mum yelling as she came bursting back through the front door and hurtled into the kitchen.

Gently plonking the box of hedgehogs on the table, she gave me a huge cuddle of a hug.

"Indie, I am *so* sorry I forgot!" I heard Mum say, though I couldn't *see* her – I was still lost in her hug.

"Thassokay," I mumbled into her

inside-out, back-to-front jumper.

"Right! *I* know! Close your eyes!"

I did what I was told, and tried to picture what all the thudding, clanking and stomping was about.

"You can open them now!"

 **PING!**

My eyes flew open, only to see Mum standing in front of me holding a birthday cake, complete with candles.

Well, OK, it was more of a slightly stale fairy cake, with one full-size candle shoved in it at a wonky angle.

But it still made me feel all fuzzy inside: Mum hadn't quite forgotten my birthday *after* all!

"I'll get you a proper birthday cake tonight, after work," Mum promised. "So come on; blow the candle out and make a wish, Indie!"

I took a step closer – *and tripped*

right over Kenneth our Scottie dog, who'd sniffed that there was cake somewhere close by.

"Gerroff!" I laughed, as I lay sprawled on the floor, with Kenneth, and then George, trying to lick me better, before Mum managed to help me up.

Well, that had been quite a good (and silly!) start to my birthday...

But if I didn't hurry up, I'd be late for school, and spending my birthday in detention wouldn't be very good at all!

2

Bad at being good

My best friends Soph (Sophie Musyoka) and Fee (Sophie Dean) didn't get a chance to make much of a birthday fuss of me *after* all.

"Indie! You're *very* late!" said my teacher, Miss Levy, when I came hurrying and hassled

20

into class. "What happened?"

Miss Levy *tried* to look stern, but didn't do a very good job of it, 'cause she's *way* too nice. Still, it was one of those moments when I felt *very* not brave, and a *whole* lot weedy.

"Um… I kind of got talking to my neighbour," I tried to explain, feeling my face burning red with running and embarrassment.

"Indie, you shouldn't really stand around chatting to neighbours when you've got school!" Miss Levy said, frowning and smiling all at once.

"Yes, I know. But it was Mrs O'Neill…" I replied lamely, wondering how I could explain how Mrs O'Neill, our very old lady neighbour, wiffles and waffles and never stops once she's got started.

Like this morning: Mrs O'Neill had stopped me as I was leaving the house to wish me happy birthday, which was very nice of her, but not when I was in such a hurry that I was even eating my breakfast (fairy cake) as I ran.

The trouble with Mrs O'Neill is that she's a bit lonely, Mum says. So it's not nice to rush her, even when she gets side-tracked and starts talking about slugs on her marigolds or the price of jam.

But before I got a chance to explain all that, Soph said: "*Please* don't tell Indie off, Miss Levy – it's her birthday today!"

I gave Soph a thank-you smile.

"Well, happy birthday, Indie," said Miss Levy. "But sit down now and let's get on with the lesson. I've already told the class this morning that I want you all to do a CV, which stands for 'curriculum vitae'."

That sounded *very* complicated. Soph thought so too; I could tell from the way she looked at me and crossed her eyes. I tried not to giggle (which made me go even redder). Fee didn't pull a face because she is very good at hard words and probably already knew what a curly lum vitty was.

"Anyway, a CV is basically just a list of your talents," Miss Levy continued.

"She means we have to write down what we're good at," Fee whispered to me, and got a shush from Miss Levy for her trouble.

"Enough with the chit-chat! Let's get on with our lists!"

Miss Levy LOVES lists, because she says they...

1) are EASY to read
2) help you get organized
3) sort out what's IMPORTANT.

"And I *know* all of my fantastic pupils have *plenty* of talents," Miss Levy called out encouragingly, as everyone shuffled around getting out exercise books and pencils. "But to make it easier, have a think and then choose only the top three things!"

I sat for a minute and realized that I couldn't think of *any* three things.

Take today, for instance... I mean, I *knew* there was stuff I liked doing – like getting up at 6 a.m. and feeding mini-hedgehogs, but that's not what you could call a talent, is it?

And I always reminded Mum about things she was too busy to remember (like mini-hedgehogs), and I had the patience to listen to Mrs O'Neill's wiffle-waffling, but both of those were just about being nice, weren't they?

Oh, *why* hadn't Miss Levy asked us to do a 'Nice Things I Don't Mind Doing' list instead of a 'Top Three Talents' one?

"What have you put down?" I

whispered in a mild panic to Soph, who was sitting at the desk to the left of me.

Soph pushed her exercise book to the edge of her desk so I could see. Her really big, whirly, swirly handwriting had already covered nearly a whole page. (EEK!)

1) I'm VERY good at Irish dancing (I won a competition last week).

2) I can speak THREE languages (English, French, Somali).

3) I can jump from the top board at the pool (and my dad is teaching me how to do a proper dive).

Soph *is* very good at Irish dancing, even though she's half-Somalian and half-French and not very Irish at all (I tried going to her dance class once, but my legs just got very confused). And she can speak *all* those languages (she taught me how to say 'sausage' in Somali and French), and she is a very good swimmer too.

Altogether, Soph's was a very good list. Which would make mine look even *more* rubbish, when I got around to writing it.

Oh, IF ONLY I could dance really well, or speak Slovak, or jump off even the *bottom* board at the pool without belly-flopping…

"What did *you* put down, Fee?" I asked, turning to the desk on my right.

"Um… I wrote: **1. Scrabble, 2. Spelling, 3. Hair**," she whispered back, not even

having to look at her work book to read out her (short) answers.

Fee has really gorgeous, long, wavy, red hair, which she is VERY, VERY proud of, even though some people are a bit funny about ginger, aren't they? But she has this really white skin and these spookily light green eyes, and when you try to imagine her with brown or black or blonde hair, it makes you realize that they'd be all wrong and the only colour hair that works is ginger.

I gave Fee a quick smile and then stared back down at the blank page open in front of me. Hardly noticing I was doing it, I started twisting one of my (mousey-brown) bunches while I thought.

And
thought.
And
thought.
And
thought,
till my head got twisty.

And then finally, when I saw Miss Levy wandering between the desks in my direction, stopping to glance at everyone's lists, I realized I'd better stick something down *fast*.

"OK, birthday girl!" She smiled down at me. "Let's have a peek at what you've got here!"

> 1) I'm sort of QUITE nice and not too annoying.
> 2) I have QUITE a nice name.
> 3) When I'm bored I count my freckles in the mirror.

Miss Levy kept smiling, but I think she was only doing that to be kind.

"Um ... well ... I guess that's a good start, Indie," Miss Levy lied kindly. "Those are all *very* interesting facts, but I'm *sure* you can think of a few more good points and talents if you try a bit harder!"

There are things you can say to teachers and things you can't.

I mean, you can't say stuff like, "Want to bet?", 'cause it would sound *way* too cheeky.

"Why don't you think about it a bit more, and get back to me with a new list, Indie?" Miss Levy suggested. "Let's see ... by the end of the week, shall we say?"

"OK!" I nodded, trying to look like that wouldn't be a problem, even if my tummy sort of *instantly* scrunched up in a worry ball as I wondered what on earth I could come up with instead.

Urghhh...

It was right then that I realized the one thing I should have wished for on my pretend birthday candle this morning ... a talent.

Anyone know where I can find one?

3

Trying out
a talent

Soph and Fee (my super-talented friends) had decided to help *me* think of a talent, which is why – on my birthday – I went round to Fee's after school, taking George and Kenneth too.

Talking about my birthday, Soph had given me a huge badge that said, *It's my birthday, hug me!*, and Fee had given me a tiara with glittery pink jewels in it.

I decided to wear them both around to Fee's, just to feel more special and properly birthday-ish. (Now *that* was an example of being very brave, and definitely not weedy.)

I got a few stares (and no hugs) on my way, but George and Kenneth weren't in the least bit embarrassed to be seen with me, mainly 'cause they were just happy to be going for a walk somewhere.

Only now, sitting in Fee's bedroom — working our way through a mountain of munchies — Kenneth was sort of embarrassing *me*...

"Er, Indie... Kenneth's doing that weird thing again," muttered Fee, who likes things to be sensible.

"Maybe Garfield just tastes good?!" suggested Soph, who likes to be silly.

"He's just grooming him. He does it to our cat Smudge too," I told them, as we watched Kenneth lick, lick, licking Fee's fat cat Garfield.

I frowned a bit at Kenneth, trying to figure out what was going on in his furry, doggy mind.

"Hey, maybe Kenneth fancies being a

hairdresser. Or should that be a fur-dresser?!" giggled Soph.

I don't suppose Kenneth really day-dreams about being a fur-dresser, but I *do* reckon that both my dogs aren't very talented at being, well, *dogs*.

I mean, for a start, Kenneth thinks he's a cat. It's not just the fact that he likes hanging out with cats; a couple of months ago Mum had to rescue him out of a tree.

And George: well, he was supposed to be a racing greyhound – but he fell asleep at the start line during the one and only race he was ever in.

(By the way, Brian our angelfish doesn't seem very good at being a fish – instead of swimming around, he spends most of his time hiding in the tank weeds. My step-brother Dylan says maybe Brian's just modest, and doesn't like to show off the fact that he's prettier than the goldfish. Dylan could be right, but he hasn't actually *seen* Brian for himself, 'cause he's not allowed to come to our house, since he's allergic to anything furry or scaly, and our house is *full* of furry, scaly things.)

"Look," said Fee, suddenly turning away from Kenneth and Garfield and staring seriously at me and Soph. "There are only five biscuits and half a packet of Quavers left and we *still* haven't come up with a talent for Indie!"

She was right.

"Maybe Indie could become a biscuit expert!" grinned Soph, holding up her half-eaten Hobnob. "We could blindfold her and make her guess which bis—"

"*I* know!" Fee said, interrupting Soph's dumb suggestion.

Me and Soph watched (and nibbled biscuits) as Fee rummaged around under her bed and brought out a box (along with big fuzzballs of dust, a dried-up felt pen and a missing sock).

"I got this as a Christmas present," said Fee, handing the box to me, "but I've never used it. Maybe you could give it a try, Indie?"

The lid of the box said,

Hours of fun with Hair Wraps!

and there was a picture of a grinning girl with loads of brightly coloured threads wound around sections of her hair.

"Give it a try, Indie!" Fee smiled. "You can practise on me!"

Suddenly, I was kind of excited. Could hair-wrapping be my talent?

Er ... first I had to work out how you got started. Call me a doughball, but all this string and twisting looked as complicated as physics, at first glance.

"Come on, pick some colours, Indie!" Soph laughed.

So I picked pale pink (to match the twinkly stones in my tiara), light blue (to match my jeans) and bright red (to match my cheeks, which were blushing 'cause I hadn't a *clue* what I was doing).

"*Tie the ends of the thread near the root of the hair*," Soph read aloud from the instruction leaflet.

"OWW!" yelped Fee.

"Sorry!" I said, blushing some more. "OK, Soph – I've done that. Now what?"

"Um… *Wrap the threads really tightly around the hair—*"

"OWW!"

"Sorry, Fee!"

"*—varying colours till you get a nice pattern!*"

For a few minutes, I bit my lip and concentrated, as Soph silently watched what I was doing. (Soph being silent is a *BAD* sign, by the way. Normally, she can chatter about all sorts of rubbish for days on end.)

"Well? How's it looking?" asked Fee.

I wanted to tell her that it was brilliant; that it was like a work of art; that everyone at school would be hassling me to do a hair wrap for them (even the boys!).

But the trouble was, Fee's hair wrap looked like a bit of old knitting that had gone very, *very* wrong.

Worse still, I'd managed to get two of my fingers knotted up in the wrap, and the tip of my middle finger was turning white, 'cause of the thread cutting off the blood supply.

"Hold on," said Soph, seeing the mess I was in and reaching over to help. "Let's give this pink thread here a *little* tug…"

"OOWWWWWWWWWWWWWW!"

"Oh! Sorry, Fee!" I said in a panic.

"Yeah, sorry, Fee!" Soph joined in, her dark eyebrows creasing together. "Indie was in a tangle and I had to— Uh-oh…!"

It was actually a very *big* case of uh-oh.

My fingers were still tangled up in the jumble of thread – but the long twist of hair wrap wasn't attached to Fee's head any more. Which – EEK! – left Fee with a small, round, bald spot where lovely ginger hair used to be! Looked like I still needed to find a talent, since I was not very good at hair-wrapping at all…

The dog disguised as a potato

"So!" said Dad, handing me a plate with a huge slice of cake on it. "What's new with you, Indie?"

I was about to tell him about yesterday's disaster with Fee's hair (she'd even-
tually forgiven me and Soph – phew!) and
my serious lack of talents (there were only
three days left before I had to get back to
Miss Levy with my list), when some
singing got in the way.

"Happy birthday to you,
happy birthday to you!"

trilled my step-mum Fiona, as she bustled
into the living room with gift-wrapped
somethings.

"Happy birthday, dear INDIE!"

Dad and Dylan joined in.

"Happy birthday to YOOOU!"

Well, to be exact, it was the day *after* my
birthday, and I was having Birthday No. 2
round at my dad's house.

"Um, thanks," I smiled, opening parcel No. 1, which contained a 'pretty' jumper with a pony's head on it. (I was trying *very* hard to sound like I was thrilled about such a horrible present, but could feel my cheeks radiating telltale I'm-fibbing blushes.)

parcel No. 1

"And that one's from *me*!" said Dylan, as I tore open present No. 2, and stared at the title of the book in my hand: *Fascinating Fossils!*

parcel No. 2

"Great!" I grinned, feeling really, truly, horribly *horrible* about fibbing.

Now it was time for parcel No. 3. (Eeek...)

"Wow! *Thank* you!" I giggled with proper, *genuine* happiness and relief, as I unwrapped a brand new mobile phone.

parcel No. 3

"It's got photo-messaging – look!" said Dylan, grabbing the phone from me and taking a snap of my birthday cake, which had been made by Fiona (she's the cookery writer for the local newspaper) and decorated with a zillion girly icing-sugar roses.

My step-mum Fiona likes girly things. She doesn't like germs, dust and messiness. I'd already spotted her frowning at a couple of stray dog hairs on my T-shirt. I bet she was worried that they'd make Dylan start sneezing or swelling up or something…

"So, what's new with you, Dad?" I asked, once Dylan had showed me how to zap my cake picture to *his* mobile (Dylan was the only other person I knew with a photo-messaging phone).

"Well, for the wedding I'm doing this week, I've bought an amazing new lens for my camera," said Dad enthusiastically. (He's a wedding photographer for the local newspaper, where he met Fiona.)

"What's so amazing about your lens thingy, then?" I asked, nibbling a bit of flowery cake *very* carefully, so that no crumbs or icing-sugar petals landed on the floor.

"It does this special multi-faceted effect!"

I must have looked totally confused, 'cause next thing, Dad zoomed off to his darkroom to get the brochure to show me.

And as Dad zoomed, Fiona gathered up his empty plate and Dylan's too, even though I didn't think Dylan was finished (his cheeks were bulging like a hamster's).

"Hey, Indie…" Dylan mumphed with his mouth full. "Have you ever seen a picture of how flies' eyes work?"

Huh?

Typical Dylan: he was always coming up with nuts stuff out of the blue, like asking if I'd ever seen a picture of how flies' eyes work when we weren't even having a conversation about flies, as far as I could remember.

Also, although Dylan was only nine

(and weird), he was so stupidly good at everything at school that sometimes he made me feel a bit … well … *stupid*.

"I think I *have* seen something like that…" I said warily, wondering what he was on about.

"With the new lens for Mike's camera" – Dylan called my dad by his first name – "the photo comes out looking like how flies see things, with everything broken up into hexagons."

"What d'you mean, exactly?" I asked, feeling thick.

"Like … like a mosaic. That's just one picture, but it's made up of loads of little pieces."

Ah, *now* I got it … the

bride would look like a jigsaw puzzle. Uh-oh…

"The people getting married aren't going to *like* that," I muttered glumly.

"I know. Your Wedding Day meets *A Bug's Life*!" Dylan giggled at his own joke.

My mouth was starting to stretch to a smile too, even though me and Dylan didn't normally have much of a sense of humour in common, *and* I was worried about Dad losing his job 'cause of taking weirdo wedding pics.

And as it turned out, I had every reason to be worried…

"Mike already had some bride moaning on the phone to him today," said Dylan, reaching over to the magazine rack and pulling out a recent copy of the local paper. "Look!"

On this week's wedding picture, Dad had snapped the photo so that you could only see the bride and groom's faces from the nose *up*.

"Oh…" I mumbled, suddenly worried that Dad might get fired from his job soon, if he didn't start taking *normal* pictures.

"Who's the dog?"

For a second, I thought that this was a very *rude* way to talk about a bride, till I realized that Dylan was looking at the opposite page, where there was a photo of my pretty blonde mum, smiling and holding the world's ugliest dog.

It was like a black blob with wonky eyes and chewed ears.

If the headline hadn't read

GIVE A DOG A HOME

I might have thought that it was a pot-bellied pig crossed with a potato.

"Dunno... I'll have to ask Mum," I replied to Dylan's question, quickly scanning the story underneath and reading that the dog was called Dib and that he'd been at the centre longer than any other animal, *including* the parrot that kept getting returned 'cause it said rude words.

"So what did you wish for, then, Indie?"

See what I meant about Dylan? He was *really* hard to have a conversation with, the way he darted from flies' eyes, to dogs that looked like potatoes, to wishes, without giving you a chance to catch up.

"*What* wish? When I blew out the candles on my cake a little while ago, you mean?" I asked.

"Uh-huh," nodded Dylan, as he reached over and pinched one of the zillions of icing-sugar roses to eat.

"Well, I…"

Well, I wasn't actually sure if I wanted to tell him what I'd wished for, in case he thought it was *way* too pathetic.

"…I wished for a talent."

Oops – it just slipped out. Like I said, I have absolutely *no* talent for lots of things, including fibbing, so I *had* to tell Dylan the truth.

"What – so you want to find something to be really good at?" he asked.

"Or just good-*ish*," I shrugged, not wanting to seem greedy.

Dylan sometimes does this thing where

he goes quiet and blinks at nothing, as if he's switched his brain off. But the absolute *opposite* is happening – it's like he's flicking through a thousand files in his mind at supersonic speed, trying to find some information.

And he was doing that now; the only sound in the silent room was the crunching of icing-sugar roses between Dylan's teeth.

"*I* know! I know the *perfect* talent you could have!"

OK, so Dylan was a weirdo, but he was the smartest weirdo I knew and I couldn't *wait* to hear what he had to say…

A handful of hedgehog

"Mum…?"

"Yep?" muttered Mum, frowning at the tiny hedgehog she'd just plucked out of the box of tiny hedgehogs. (She was trying to figure out which mini-hedgehog was which, and who'd been fed already.)

"When I was round at Dad's today—"

I was about to ask Mum about the dog that me and Dylan saw her with in the paper.

"Yeah ... you told me. Dylan suggested something you could try, as a talent," muttered Mum distractedly, narrowing her eyes as she gently placed the hedgehog into my cupped hands.

"Yeah, right. Magic tricks," I mumbled, allowing myself to get side-tracked, as the gorgeously cute hedgehog wriggled and tickled against my palms.

But I mean, *magic* tricks.

So much for Dylan being *smart*.

His idea for a talent was even *more* useless than hair wraps...

"So what's wrong with magic tricks? You could've used that birthday money I gave you to buy yourself a beginner's kit, Indie. Didn't you fancy giving that a try?"

"No *way*! Magic's boring!" I laughed, backing onto the kitchen stool and nearly sitting on Smudge. (Smudge didn't seem to notice, but then our cat sleeps so much she's probably awake as often as your average cushion.)

"Magic's not *boring*," Mum laughed. "Those blokes on TV can do amazing stuff, like making helicopters disappear!"

"Yeah, but *normal* magic's just stuff like card tricks," I tried to explain, remembering a really dull kids' entertainer Soph had had at her eighth birthday party. "I mean, if I could learn how to turn kittens into Siberian tigers, or make Fee's bald spot disappear, then that would be *very* cool. But *card* tricks? I don't think so…"

"So you still need to find a talent then?" Mum smiled.

"Yes, please…"

You bet. It was Wednesday already,

and I only had till the end of the week to come up with my top three talents for Miss Levy.

"Well, what about star signs?"

"Star signs?"

For a second, I wondered why on earth Mum had thought of that, and then I noticed the torn-out magazine page that was lining the plastic hedgehog box. On the part that wasn't covered in bedding or hedgehog wee, you could clearly read the words:

Your horoscopes for the week.

"But I don't know anything *about* that stuff!" I told Mum.

"Yes, but maybe you could read up and find out what different star signs are meant to be like – and then try guessing what signs people are. *That'd* be fun!"

Before I could mull over that *maybe-*talent, the phone rang.

"I'll get it!" I told Mum, since she had more hedgehogs than me to look after. "Hello?"

"Did the picture in the paper work? Has Dib got a home yet?"

It was Dylan, not even bothering to waste time with *hi* or *hello*.

I knew everything happened very quickly in his brainy brain, but as we were only looking through the newspaper together round at his place half an hour ago, I couldn't see how Dib would have found a loving new owner that quickly.

"I'll ask Mum," I told him, since he sounded so keen to know. (Actually, I was keen to know too, which is why I started quizzing her about it a little while ago.)

"What's up?" Mum asked, looking up from her feeding and sorting.

"Tell her it's Dylan," said Dylan.

"It's Dylan," I said to Mum.

"Tell her we saw her photo in the paper today and—"

"We saw your photo in the paper today and Dylan wants to know if that funny-looking dog Dib has got a home yet."

"Dib?" Mum frowned.

"Oh, you mean the **DIB**!"

Did I?

"Appparently, at the first rescue centre he was in, someone decided to call him **DIB**, because **DIB** is short for **Dog In Black** like the movie *Men In Black*!"

I was totally confused. There I was, talking to my ditzy step-brother on the phone, holding a conker-sized hedgehog, and listening to my mum speaking in code.

HELP!

"What does she mean, 'the first rescue centre he was in'?" Dylan asked in my ear.

"What d'you mean, 'the first rescue centre he was in'?" I asked Mum.

"Well, we're his third. He spent months in the first two rescue centres, and no one chose to re-home him, so he came to us."

"Mum says he spent months—"

"I heard," Dylan interrupted me. "Poor dog!"

Poor dog all right; it wasn't just a **DIB** – it was a **DIBWAVU**. (Dog In Black Who's Also Very Ugly). No wonder the first two centres had found it hard to get him a new owner.

"But back to Dylan's first question," said Mum. "No, the **DIB** hasn't got a home yet. Doesn't Dylan fancy having a dog?"

"Can't," Dylan sighed in my ear. "Allergies, remember?"

"Can't – he's allergic," I repeated to Mum.

(I was starting to get a scrambled brain with this three-way conversation.)

"Oh, yes... I forgot. Pity." Mum shrugged, lifting the mewling hedgehog back out of my hands now that she'd worked out which conker-head was which.

"OK, see ya," Dylan mumbled, super-keen to get off the phone all of a sudden.

"Hold on a sec, Dyl!" I said, before he disappeared on me. "Can I, er, ask you something?"

A dumb idea had just flashed into my dumb head.

"Uh ... yeah, OK. What?"

"Can I ... er ... can I try to guess your

star sign?"

Mum instantly glanced up from the hedgehogs and grinned encouragingly.

"Um ... I s'pose so," muttered Dylan.

"Well," I began, concentrating hard(ish) and trying to turn all psychic. "I bet you're ... a Pisces!"

"No."

"Um ... Capricorn?"

"No."

"Scorpio, then?"

"No."

"Er ... Sagittarium?"

Mum was shaking her head madly and I knew I'd goofed.

"Indie, there's no such sign as Sagittarium!" know-all Dylan told me.

"OK, I give up," I sighed, realizing that I didn't know any more star signs or even how many there were in the zodiac (whatever a 'zodiac' was). "So what star sign *are* you?"

"Well, my birthday was two weeks ago, so I'm Libra, same as you," said Dylan.

Oh.

So maybe guessing star signs wasn't the right talent for me either, specially since I hadn't even known what my own star sign was till now.

Oops...

6

The sardine-scented comfort blankie

I'd decided to give the horoscope thing a proper go, seeing as I didn't have any other talents to try, and *specially* because it was Thursday afternoon already and Miss Levy expected a brand new, improved CV on her desk first thing tomorrow.

So, I was going to try out my star sign skills in a second; I just had to do a quick something first...

Click!

The **DIB** didn't move as I held my brand new photo-messaging phone up and snapped in his direction. He was looking at me kind of blankly.

He *kept* looking at me kind of blankly as I zapped his picture to Dylan (at least Dylan wasn't allergic to *pictures* of animals).

The **DIB** stared dopily as I put my phone away and started flicking through the horoscope book I'd borrowed from the school library at lunchtime today.

"OK, how about this: *Those born under the sign of Taurus*," I began to read aloud, "*love their home comforts...*"

Glancing up, I checked out the fat, black blob sitting in the corner of a concrete pen, with the edge of a mucky-looking bit of blanket in its mouth.

"*They also love their food...*"

One empty stainless-steel food bowl, one fat blob of a dog.

"...*and can be stubborn*. Here, boy! C'mere!"

The **DIB** looked me up and down (and round a bit) with its wonky eyes, but didn't move a lumpy muscle.

"How are you getting on?" asked Mum, flippity-flapping up beside me in her rubbery green wellies.

"OK," I said. "I just tried to figure out the **DIB**'s star sign – and I think he's a Taurus!"

"I think you say 'Taurean'. But well done!" Mum grinned. "Now, how are you going to figure out if you're right, Indie? 'Cause remember, the **DIB** *is* a stray and we've got no idea how old he is, or when his birthday is!"

Drat. And there was yet *another* possible talent, disappearing into thin air like a burst soapy bubble…

"Anyway," Mum carried on regardless, pulling a clunking set of keys off her belt-loop. "Want to come and meet him properly?"

"Definitely!" I said, as I watched Mum unlock the door of the **DIB**'s pen and motion me to go in.

Hey, it's one of the perks of being a kid, isn't it? Taking advantage of the jobs your parents do, I mean.

We did a poll in class once, to decide whose parent had the best job, and *everyone* voted for Rohana, 'cause her parents ran a newsagent's and she got ALL the crisps or sweets that were out of date for NOTHING!

I got voted second (hooray!), 'cause I could go to the rescue centre *any* time I wanted and pat *anything* I wanted.

(Bottom of the list was Wesley, whose dad was an electrician. What perks could Wes get? A bag of electricity? A free electric shock?!)

"Hello!" I mumbled softly, as I stepped into the pen and crouched down in front of the black blob.

The **DIB** hardly blinked.

"Anyone *in* there?" I asked, waving a hand in front of his eyes.

No wonder this dog hadn't got a home yet – not only was he a **DIBWAVU**, but he didn't seem to have much personality either.

"I think he's just shy," said Mum from the doorway of the pen, as I reached a hand out to pat him.

And then – spookily – as soon as my hand stroked his rough fur, I heard something *odd*.

"What's that knock-knocking?" I asked Mum, although it wasn't so much a knock-knocking sound as a **thudda-dudda-dudda** sound.

"I don't know," said Mum, coming over and crouching down beside me.

And then I realized it wasn't so much a

thudda-
dudda-
dudda–

sound

as a

short,

fat

tail,

slapping on the concrete floor.

"Awww … d'you like that, doggie?"

"*Hmmmmuuurrrumff … hummumff …*"

That funny humming noise – I think it meant yes. And I could also see that the **DIB** was drooling with happiness from the corner of his mouth that wasn't hidden behind his grotty blankie.

"What if I do *that*?" I said, giving him a scratch between the shoulder blades.

"Humma... hummmmmuuurrrumff...
mmmnumff..." **FLOOP!**
The way the **DIB** suddenly fell over
was as graceful as a warthog doing
the splits.

At first I thought he'd fainted, or
maybe even *died* on me, but then I heard
that familiar **thudda-dudda-dudda-**
ing again, and saw that he'd raised his
short, stubby legs up so I could rub his sur-
prisingly pink, podgy tummy.

"You're really quite cute, aren't you?"

I smiled at him – and then caught a whiff of his blankie and nearly fainted myself.

"His blankie *really* stinks!" I moaned, wondering how a small, scruffy bit of material could smell so much of boiled cabbage and sardines.

"Yeah, he was found with that blankie when he was picked up originally, and he gets *really* upset if you try to take it away from him," Mum explained. "But something that smelly doesn't really help get a new owner interested in him."

The poor **DIB** – his comfort blankie wasn't the *only* problem. If you were walking past his pen and saw him sitting motionless in the corner like *I'd* done when I first arrived, you'd probably mistake him for a half-filled black bin liner…

Actually, I'd suddenly been hit – splat!
– by a good idea.

"I'm going to do a CV for him!" I told Mum excitedly. "You know, a list of all his good points! And you can pin it to the outside of his pen, so that anyone passing can read it and find out more about him!"

"Hmm…" mumbled Mum, raising her eyebrows thoughtfully. "And what good points are you going to write about exactly?"

Ooh, that *was* tough.

© Can sit VERY still for ages.
© Can make his eyeballs LOOK
   in two different directions at
   the same time.
© Makes a funny humming sound
   when you scratch his head.

None of that sounded like much of a talent. Which reminded me, that new list of talents for Miss Levy was due first thing in the morning.

I didn't know which list of talents was going to be harder to write: the **DIB**'s or mine.

(Although at least I didn't look like a potato, I hoped!)

A whole bunch of trouble

"Do you think Miss Levy was *really* cross with me?" I asked Soph and Fee, as we strolled around the mini-zoo in the park on Saturday morning.

It's horrible if you're worried that your favourite teacher thinks you're as annoying as a snotty cold, isn't it?

"Indie, you've asked us that seventeen trillion times," grinned Soph, as she licked her ice cream. "She wasn't cross, she was

just a bit ... *sigh*-y!"

"'Sigh-y' isn't a proper word!" Fee corrected her.

"Whatever," shrugged Soph, hopping to one side as two little kids hurtled after a pygmy goat, trying to pet it. "You know what I mean. Anyway, Miss Levy couldn't have been too cross with you yesterday, Indie – she gave you till Monday to come up with your list of tal—"

Soph got stopped in mid-word by a strange noise.

It wasn't the OINK of a pot-bellied pig.

It wasn't the HOOT of a cockatoo.

It wasn't EE-AW of a donkey.

It was the HOWL of my daft dog, Kenneth, who – like George – had to wait tied up by his lead at the zoo gate.

"Meeeee-hooooow!"

"That is the *weirdest* doggy howl I've ever heard!" giggled Soph.

She was right. If I had to do a CV for Kenneth, it'd say...

1) thinks he's a cat
2) acts like a cat
3) starting to sound like a cat.

I was getting very good at CVs now (only not for myself, of course). The one I'd done for the **DIB** turned out really well, in the end. I'd written...

STOP!!!

Please don't pass me by. Here are some things you need to know about me:

1) I don't have a proper name – I just get called the **DIB** (Dog In Black).

2) I know I'm not very pretty, but I can't help it.

3) If I seem a bit quiet, it's 'cause I'm VERY, VERY shy.

4) I love cuddles, but no one wants to give me any.

5) I can make my eyes **LOOK** in two different directions at once – see?!

6) I can make a really good noise with my tail when I'm happy – listen!

Will you be my friend?

Love and **(thudda-dudda)** tail wags,

The DIB

"Poor Kenneth," I said, trying not to listen to his sad **mee-howling**. "He doesn't know why he can't come in here with all the other animals!"

"I bet there's a queue of people out there staring at him, thinking he's the zoo's new special attraction," said Fee. "A cross between a cat and a dog!"

"A cadog!" sniggered Soph. "Or even a dogat!!"

Meeeee-haaaaow

"Don't be silly!" I butted in. "Kenneth's just your plain, ordinary, standard *nutter* dog!"

Poor Kenneth. If only he could understand human-speak and hear me, Soph and Fee laughing at his expense. He'd probably bite our ankles – either that, or deliberately give us his fleas.

"Hey … talking about weird dogs," said Fee, as we all giggled our way over to the donkeys' paddock. "Did your special CV help that Dib dog get a new owner yet?"

"Not yet," I replied, shaking my head. "But Mum said most people visit the rescue centre at the weekends, so I'm keeping my fingers crossed."

I wasn't the *only* one keeping my fingers crossed for the **DIB** – Dylan had texted me to say he wouldn't just keep his fingers crossed but his toes too, which might make *walking* a bit tricky...

"Y'know, you're *so* GOOD with animals, Indie – you're just like your mum!" said Fee, resting her elbows on the fence around the paddock.

I turned to say thanks for the compliment, but then came over all embarrassed and weedy and just said

mmmmff!

instead.

"Here, little donkey! Want some ice cream?" asked Soph, holding her cone out towards the grey-brown donkey ambling towards us.

"Don't listen to her!" I called out, ushering the donkey towards me instead. "You're not supposed to eat ice cream. It's bad for you!"

The donkey stopped, flicked its ears like it was listening to me, then clip-clopped in my direction.

"Cool!" laughed Soph, not in the least bit offended that her offer of ice cream had been turned down. "You'd think it knew what you were saying, Indie!"

"Hey, Indie – maybe you're like Dr Doolittle!" said Fee excitedly. "You know. The guy in that story who can talk to animals!"

Maybe Fee's right! I thought, as the donkey nuzzled its damp, rubbery nose into my hand.

Maybe I *could* be like Dr Doolittle and talk to animals.

Maybe *that* could be my talent?!

"Say something else to it, Indie!" Soph encouraged me.

I wanted to, but what?

"Um, hello…" I muttered softly, practically going cheek to hairy cheek with the donkey. "Do you understand me?"

wumph

"Wumph," the donkey wumphed, its breath smelling of apple and hay and carrots.

"If you can understand me, then flick your tail once for ye—"

I'd hardly finished saying the word "yes" when I heard either Soph or Fee give a surprised shriek.

Wow ... it must have worked! They must have seen the donkey flick its tail!

I tried to turn my head to ask them – and...

OOOOOF!

…suddenly found myself *jerked* back.

"Washappenin'!!" I mumbled at high speed.

The sudden OOOOOF-y head-jerking *wasn't* a nice feeling, and I didn't really like the sound of all that munching either…

"*Naughty* donkey! Let *go*!!" I heard Fee flapping about, though I couldn't turn my head enough to see her.

"Oh *no*!! It's eating one of your bunches, Indie!" I heard (and saw) Soph squeal.

"Make it stop!" I begged whichever one of my friends might make that happen.

"Quick, Soph!" Fee said urgently. "Try to tempt it away with your ice cream!"

I didn't know if that was going to work, but out of the corner of my eye, I could see one of the zookeepers rushing over to help.

I tried *not* to notice all the mums and dads and kids pointing and giggling at me. And I tried *not* to think about the fact that talking to animals was something I was very, very untalented at.

"*Meeeee-hooooow!!*"

At the sound of Kenneth's distant miaow/howl, I wished upon wish upon *wish* that I was safe at home with the dogs and Mum and the baby hedgehogs, instead of here at the zoo, being a mid-morning snack for a donkey with the munchies...

Dylan's dead-good idea

"Why does your hair look weird, Indie?" said Dylan, walking into the kitchen and plonking himself down on a stool at the other side of the breakfast bar to me.

"Hi, Dylan!" I answered him, remembering my manners, even if my step-brother didn't see the point of them.

It was Sunday and I was round at Dad's for lunch, even though Dad was nowhere

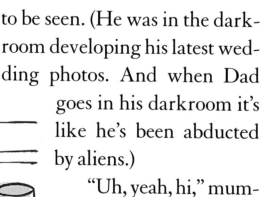

to be seen. (He was in the dark-room developing his latest wedding photos. And when Dad goes in his darkroom it's like he's been abducted by aliens.)

"Uh, yeah, hi," mumbled Dylan, giving me a vague wave hello.

"So why does your hair look weird?"

"A donkey ate it," I told him, tugging self-consciously at the slightly shorter bunch. "Why?"

"'Cause I was trying to talk to it. I thought talking to animals would

93

be a good talent to have, but it didn't work out."

"Oh," said Dylan. "So, did the **DIB** get a new home yet?"

I don't think Dylan meant to be rude; it was just that his faster-than-average brain was skipping on to the next subject already.

"Not yet," I shrugged. "But Mum said a lot of people mentioned the notice, so that's good. Maybe someone will—"

"Hey, you could do a poster, Indie!" Dylan butted in again. "You could do a poster with a picture on and everything. And you could put it up somewhere where lots of people would see it!"

"Where? Like on a tree, you mean? Sort of like a 'Lost Cat' poster?"

Dylan shook his head at me.

"Not enough people would see it on a

tree. Is there a noticeboard at your school?"

"Yes ... there is!" I nodded, getting a rush of excitement at Dylan's dead-good idea.

Which faded away in a second when I thought of a problem.

"But how do you do a proper poster with a photo and everything?"

"If you wrote the words, then I could design it on my computer!" Dylan offered. "And I could use that photo you sent me on your mobile!"

I'd forgotten that Dylan was a nine-year-old whizz-kid on the computer. It wouldn't surprise me if he designed a best-selling computer game by the time he was my age and became a multi-trillion-aire by the time he was twelve...

And so me and Dylan worked on his dead-good idea all Sunday afternoon, and first thing on Monday, I stuck the finished poster up on the noticeboard at school.

"I'm glad you had fun doing that project with your step-brother over the weekend, Indie, but I wish you'd taken time to do that assignment I gave you!" said Miss Levy, once I got to class and tried to give her my lame excuses.

"I'll do it for tomorrow – promise!" I said, feeling my cheeks turn pink.

Miss Levy might have been a bit sigh-y again about me not doing my list, but I was still glad I'd done the poster with Dylan.

For the next hour – while we were supposed to be concentrating on Viking history – I couldn't help daydreaming about the poster and hoping someone at school would see it and give the **DIB** a home, since no one had offered him one over the weekend.

And the poster *was* ACE; I'd worked really hard getting the words *just* right, and then Dylan had got this symbol of a hand pointing and placed it next to the photo I'd taken of the **DIB** – *that* looked pretty cute and funny. And then he'd picked all this really interesting lettering that makes you want to go right up and read what it says.

Briiiiinnnnnnnggggg…!!

"Aaaa*chooo*! OK, everyone – you can go," said Miss Levy, waving us all off to

aaaachaaa

break with her soggy tissue.

(She was too busy sniffling and sneezing all of a sudden to notice that most of us were practically halfway out of the room and down the corridor already.)

"I don't think I like the Vikings," muttered Fee, as we strolled together. "All they do is fight and wear silly pointy hats!"

"I know! Why can't we do the history of boy bands instead?" suggested Soph.

"Or the history of crisps?" I chipped in.

We'd just decided that the history of crisps would be totally excellent (as long as we could eat lots of different types for homework) when we all spotted a scrum around the noticeboard.

"Your poster, Indie!" said Soph excitedly. "*That* must be what everyone's looking at!"

My tummy did a quick flip – was my ad for the **DIB** going to work? Actually, maybe doing ads (with Dylan's help) was something I was talented at! Maybe when I was older, I could get a job at Cadbury's and make brilliant TV ads for Chocolate Buttons and stuff…

"What's up with that lot?" Fee frowned,

when a ripple of laughter suddenly wafted our way.

I started speeding up – like Soph and Fee – towards the crowd of sniggerers staring at my poster.

"What's going on here?" we heard Miss Levy say loudly, in a slightly croaky voice, as she click-clacked along the corridor.

As if by magic, everyone trickled away at high speed, giving me, Soph, Fee and Miss Levy a clear view of the noticeboard.

Oh.

Oh no.

Oh *no*!

Please don't let this have happened (except – duh! – it *has*).

"Oh, dear. I'll have to report this to the headteacher!" Miss Levy tut-tutted, staring at my poster.

Me, Soph and Fee didn't say anything – we were all too totally stunned.

"Are you all right, Indie?" Miss Levy turned and asked me, giving me a pat on the shoulder.

I wished she wouldn't do that, 'cause I thought I might just *blub*, I was so upset…

"Never mind. It was a good idea to put a poster up," said Miss Levy, patting my shoulder again. "I think everyone in the school should be using this noticeboard more often – it normally only has the fire regulations pinned to it. But maybe I'll suggest to the headteacher that there should be a glass front on it, so no one can vandalize anything like they've done here!"

Any other time, it would be pretty nice to get a compliment from Miss Levy, but I didn't feel too chuffed right then.

Not when I was staring at a photo of the **DIB** with a moustache, specs and devil horns drawn on in felt pen...

Tricks
in a tangle

"I thought you said magic was boring?" said Dylan, rummaging through the box of tricks I'd brought round to Dad's to practise.

"Yeah, but I'm getting desperate to find a talent, so I thought I'd give it a go," I shrugged, watching Dylan hold a plastic tube to his eye and stare at me through it.

I'd bought the magic set yesterday

after school to cheer myself up, after what happened to the **DIB**'s poster. I guess I'd kind of half-hoped there'd be a spell in there to punish vandals. But it was just full of stuff called '*Mystery Tubes*' and '*The Disappearing Ring*' and '*Phantasmagorical Fingers*'.

"Are you any good at it yet?" asked Dylan.

"Haven't tried any of it out. When I got home yesterday, Mum said her boss at the rescue centre had asked me to make up more CV thingies for some of the other hard-to-home animals, so I did that last night instead."

And – oops – forgot to do my list for Miss Levy again. But luckily (for me, not Miss Levy), she was off with a bad cold today.

"Which animals?" asked Dylan, looping a short piece of rope around his fingers.

"The parrot that says rude stuff. And an iguana whose scales have fallen off."

*pieces of *!!***

"What did you write for the swearing parrot?" asked Dylan, picking up the instruction sheet.

"Don't!" I told him, taking the instructions and the rope out of his hands. "It's supposed to be *my* talent, OK?"

Dylan just shrugged, and didn't get annoyed at that. He probably realized – same as I did – that he could do every single trick in the box better than me, if he put his mind to it.

"So what *did* you write for the parrot, though?" Dylan persisted.

"I said that he was very chatty, but that he's unsuitable for very little kids," I explained, folding the instruction sheet up neatly and making a total, scrunched-up mess of it.

"A sort of PG-rated parrot, then?" said

Dad, wandering into the kitchen, where we were sitting, and catching the end of our conversation.

"Sort of." I smiled at Dad, thinking that he was looking a bit down in the dumps today.

"So … magic tricks, eh?" said Dad, trying hard to smile back at me. "I could do with seeing a few magic tricks to cheer me up!"

"Photos," Dylan mouthed at me, and nodded his head towards the latest copy of the local newspaper.

Straight away I guessed what was wrong; yet another bride and groom hadn't liked the weirdy, bug's-eye-view snaps that poor old Dad had taken of their big day, and told him so…

"OK, Dad!" I said, nodding. "I'll do some magic tricks for you!"

"Fanatastic!" said Dad. "Well, let's see them now – Fiona says tea's not going to be ready for a while yet!"

WIBBLE.

That's the feeling I suddenly got inside,

knowing I had to perform, even though I hadn't had a chance to practise yet. (Gulp.)

Two minutes later, after a quick read of the instructions, I asked Dad, Fiona and Dylan to sit on the sofa – and to promise *not* to laugh if I messed up.

"This first trick is called '*Mystery Tubes*'," I said out loud, then felt myself blushing when they all clapped.

Uh-oh … the mystery of the '*Mystery Tubes*' was how the stupid trick *worked*.

There were two plastic see-through tubes that you put inside each other, and you were meant to poke a silk hankie through them and make one disappear.

Only I didn't *have* a silk hankie. So I was using a bit of kitchen roll instead, and suddenly, as I tried to shove the kitchen roll through, I ended up with the plastic tubes **wedged** on two of my fingers.

Yay!

Only a lot of tugging (and no magic) set me free.

"Yay!" shouted Fiona a bit too loudly, as she clapped her hands at my lousy attempt at a trick. (Or maybe she was just clapping Dylan for yanking the tubes off for me.)

"This one … um … should be better," I told my audience of three. "It's called 'The Disappearing Ring'."

OK, the trick with this was that you put a silver ring in a box and made it vanish by turning the box over so the ring was hidden under a false bottom.

All set, I turned the box over, said

"Shazam!!!"

and then opened the box a bit too hard, breaking the plastic hinges. The lid, false bottom and ring all tumbled onto the living-room floor.

"Nice try!" Fiona called out. (She is SUCH a good liar.)

"Er ... this one's called '*Phantasmagorical Fingers*'," I mumbled, too embarrassed to look at Dylan or Dad, I was making such a mess of things.

And it looked like I was going to make a mess of this trick too.

Slowly, I read the 14 diagrams that showed me how to wrap a piece of rope in an intricate pattern around my fingers. Then – hey presto! – with one tug, the rope was supposed to slip away, knot-free!

Knot *likely*.

When I gave a tug on the end of the rope, instead of gasping as it fell easily away, my Dad, Dylan and Fiona started giggling so

much they could hardly breathe, while I stuggled to untangle my knotted-up fingers.

GOOD GRIEF. I was rotten at hair-wrapping, I sucked at guessing star signs, I was terrible at talking to animals, I'd never make it in advertising and now I was minging at magic.

"Oh, Indie!" gasped Dad, laughing so much he was crying. "Thank you, honey — you really cheered me up today!"

Even if I was a bit embarrassed at being so awful, I was still pretty glad that being *bad* at doing magic tricks had put my dad in a better mood.

But being bad wasn't a talent, was it...?

Ouch!

Ding dong!

As soon as the doorbell rang, the pets went mental, just like they always do. George was jumping around the hall like a puppy on a pogo stick, Kenneth was **meeeee-hoooow**-ling for all he was worth, and Smudge the cat had woken up and then gone straight back to sleep again, doing her cushion impersonation.

"Can you get that, Indie?" Mum called

from the kitchen, where she was mixing up milky gloop for the hedgehogs' tea.

"Yep – no problem!" I called back, while trying to shush Kenneth and get George far enough away from the door so I could open it.

"What's *that*?" asked Dylan, standing halfway down our path when I finally managed to pull the front door open.

I figured out what he was looking at.

"A baby hedgehog," I grinned, holding out my cupped hand. "Want to see?"

"No, better not," he said, taking an allergic step backward.

"So what's *that*?" I asked him in turn, nodding down at the gift-wrapped box he must have dumped on the doorstep just now. (George and Kenneth were sniffing at it madly.)

"It's for you!" Dylan shrugged, backing away some more.

"What is it?" I asked him, just as I spotted Fiona, who was smiling and waving from the safety of her car.

"Mum thought you'd like it!" said Dylan, easing his way out of our gate, and away from the general allergic-ness of our house. "Got to go – got my maths club!"

And so ten seconds later, I was sitting at

the kitchen table, pulling open the parcel with a mildly curious Mum peering over my shoulder.

"A badge-making kit?" Mum frowned,

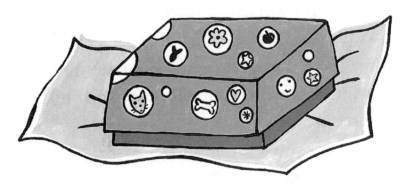

while feeding the first of the hedgehogs with a dripper full of vitamin-spiked milk. "That's very sweet of Fiona to give that to you. But what's it for? Is it a late birthday present or something?"

"She says…" I mumbled, while reading the note that came with it,

Sorry the magic tricks didn't work out

— but saw this in the shops today and thought it might be the perfect talent for you! Fiona xxx

I felt a bit mushy inside – that was really, really nice of Fiona. She wasn't bad for a step-mum, even if she *did* think pets were poisonous.

"Hey, that looks like a lot of fun!" Mum smiled, as I pulled out the badge-making machine and started fiddling with it.

But Mum was wrong.

'Cause twenty minutes and a bit of badge-making later, I was in hospital…

SAFETY ADVICE FOR BADGE WEARERS

Badges should be worn:

✚ on T-shirts

✚ on jackets

✚ on bags

✚ on hats even.

Badges should NOT be worn:

✚ on fingers...

"How did you manage to do this, then, Indie?" the nurse asked, as she gently tried to unpin the badge from my finger.

I couldn't exactly answer – I was gritting my teeth too hard.

"She had an idea about helping to find a home for a dog at the animal rescue centre I work at," Mum explained, tucking something she thought was a hair behind her ear (I think it was actually a bit of

hedgehog bedding).

"Must be a special dog!" the nurse said to me. "And how was the badge supposed to help it find a home?"

I dared to sneak a peek at what she was doing, and saw that I wasn't wearing the badge on my finger any more (phew).

The nurse was now wiping my finger with cold, wet cotton wool that smelled strong and chemically.

"I thought I'd make up a whole load of badges," I began to babble. "I was going to put a picture of the **DIB** – that's what the dog's called – on them, and print the phone number for the rescue centre and everything. I was going to hand them out to people on the street!"

"Well, nice idea, but I think you'd better stay away from badges from now on!" grinned the nurse.

"Doesn't look like badge-making will be your new talent after all!" Mum smiled ruefully at me.

"A talent? You mean a hobby, don't you?" asked the nurse, as she put a fancy plaster around my finger.

"You could say that," Mum said to the nurse, while giving my knee a squeeze. "She's on the hunt for something to be good at."

The nurse looked at me and did that smiling/frowning thing where it's hard to know if someone's being nice to you or trying to let you know they think you're an idiot (or both).

"Maybe you should try origami," she said. "*That* could be a good talent to have – it's a lot less dangerous than playing around with sharp pins!"

Perhaps the nurse was right.

Perhaps origami *would* be the perfect talent for me.

I'd just have to look it up in the dictionary or ask Fee what it *meant* first…

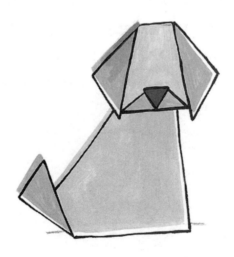

11

Nattering with Mrs O'Neill

Is 'origami'...
a) the Japanese art of paper-folding?
b) the Thai art of tummy-tickling?
c) the Chinese art of kitten-juggling?

I didn't know that the answer was a) till Mum explained on the way home. ("It's like making a paper plane," she'd said, "only fancier!")

"Origami!" I've got a magazine *all* about that!" said Mrs O'Neill. "Stay right there, Indie, and I'll get it for you!"

Mrs O'Neill had been out dusting her hedge (ie looking for someone to talk to) when Mum and I got back from the hospital.

And as soon as we'd mentioned what had happened, she wanted to hear *every* single detail, which was when I told her about the nurse suggesting I tried origami as my talent.

So me and Mum waited, and waited, and waited some more, till Mrs O'Neill rushed back out with some old magazines in her arms.

"Now, which one is it…" Mrs O'Neill muttered, rifling through the pile of old magazines that she was now balancing on top of her wheelie bin. "Ah, no, this one's **HOW TO MAKE A MACRAMÉ OWL**…"

I didn't know what macramé meant (made out of crumbs?), but I didn't think I'd ask – we'd been chatting to Mrs O'Neill for ages now and, nice as she was, I really *did* want to go home at some point this week.

"Ah! *Here* it is!" she called out, pulling out and passing me the right magazine at last. "Now look – *there's* where it tells you how to make a paper swan!"

"Thank you," I said, wondering how on earth anyone could make a flat piece of paper look *anything* like the complicated picture in the magazine.

"Thank you, Mrs O'Neill," Mum smiled, while nudging me to start moving. "Well, we'd better get Indie home, after her eventful day!"

"Oh, already?" said Mrs O'Neill, looking disappointed.

"'Fraid so!" Mum smiled kindly at her. "And we really *must* get back and feed all the animals!"

"Ah, pets … they're wonderful things – you're never without a friend when there's a pet in the house!" nodded Mrs O'Neill, getting back to dusting her hedge…

An hour later, after we'd fed George, Kenneth, Smudge, the fish, the hedgehogs, Caitlin and us, I should have been sitting down to do my CV, just in case Miss Levy's cold had got better and she was back at school tomorrow, expecting me to hand it in.

But instead, I was practising my origami.

"Ouch!" I gasped, as yet another paper cut pinched at my fingers.

I gingerly picked up my handiwork and decided to go through to the kitchen and ask Mum's opinion of it. *And* ask her where the plasters were...

"...hmm, I suppose," Mum was muttering into the phone that was tucked in between her ear and her shoulder, as she mixed up a batch of hedgehog gloop in a bowl for the night feeds. "But he's only been with us for just over a week. Should we be this quick to judge?"

Who is she talking about? I wondered, my fingers nipping.

"OK." Mum nodded at whoever was on the other end of the phone. "Let's talk in the morning. Bye."

Mum looked very serious all of a sudden. I felt a bit stupid holding up my squashed paper splodge for her to admire.

"What's up?" I asked, pulling out a stool, and checking it for snoozing cats before I sat down.

"Oh, it's just my boss." Mum shrugged. "He says he's heard there's a spare place come up at a kennels in the north. He thinks we should send the **DIB** there this weekend."

"What sort of kennels?" I asked warily, clocking how much Mum was frowning.

"Well, it's a wonderful place," said Mum, with an expression on her face that was *anything* but wonderful. "It's a long-term home for dogs that are too wild, or too institutionalized to go into a normal home."

"What does 'insti…', 'insti-wotsit' mean?"

"Dogs that have lived in rescue centres like ours for too long. They just forget how to behave in a normal house, and can't go back into one," said Mum sadly. "I had hoped it might not be too late for the **DIB**, but I suppose my boss *does* have a point, and if there *is* a place for him…"

Mum's voice tapered off, and mine wouldn't even start up.

How could the rescue centre even *think* of giving up on the **DIB** already? Of *course* he could fit into a home – sitting by someone's fire, getting his head rubbed, making his funny humming sound and **thudda-dudding** his tail … he'd be in heaven!

"So … what's *that* supposed to be?" Mum asked me out of the blue, as my brain whirred madly and miserably.

"A swan," I mumbled, holding up my scrunched-paper splodge.

"Ah, yes of course!" Mum laughed. "I can see that now – if I cross my eyes!

"I don't think I'm very good at origami," I sighed, aiming my crumpled something at the bin, and picturing the **DIB**'s dumb, squashy face.

"Still, it was very sweet of Mrs O'Neill to look out that magazine for you. And I really like the way you take time to talk to her, Indie – she's lonely, and does appreciate the company."

Frooooom!

That was the sound of an idea darting into my head faster than a paper swan flapping its wings at high speed.

And that idea was black and blob-shaped. Oh, yes; the amazing idea I'd just had might mean that the **DIB** *didn't* have to go into the Home For Wild Or Insti-wotsit Dogs.

And it could mean that he and Mrs O'Neill need *never* be lonely again…!

12

Indie to the rescue!

Brrrrrinnnnggg!

Hurray! That was the end-of-day bell, and I couldn't *wait* to rush round to Mrs O'Neill's and see how she was getting on with the **DIB**.

(Mrs O'Neill had taken a bit of persuading. So had Mum. But last night, the two of them had had a chat on their own and agreed that a trial visit from the **DIB** was worth a go. And that trial visit was happening TODAY!)

"Indie! Can I have a quick word please?"

Drat, I was in for another telling-off.

"Yes, Miss Levy?" I blinked, feeling myself go pink.

Soph and Fee threw me sympathetic glances as they filed out of the room with the rest of the class.

"Indie, you're normally a very good pupil, which is why I'm going to give you one last chance to do the CV exercise I set you," said Miss Levy. "It's Thursday now, so I'm going to let you have another whole weekend to do it. All right?"

Miss Levy looked very stern, but it was kind of hard to take her seriously, since her nose was red as a beetroot 'cause of her cold.

"Yes," I said, nodding frantically. "But I *have* been trying really hard to find talents!"

"Indie, I don't think you need to find them. I'm sure you've got plenty already!" sighed Miss Levy, putting her hands on her hips.

OK, so now I was pinker still, thanks to her compliment.

Before I could mumble to her that I didn't think so, she had a sneezing fit. So I took the opportunity to say, "OKthankyouMissLevy-bye!!" very quickly and ran out of the classroom, past a waving Soph and Fee, and all the way home, till I had to slow down in our road 'cause I was so out of breath.

Wonder if they've made friends yet? Wonder if Mrs O'Neill's heard the DIB doing that humming thing? I thought, as I saw Mrs O'Neill's house come into view.

"Help! NO!"

Uh-oh. Where was that shouting coming from?

 "No, no, no, no, *no*!"

 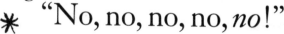

I didn't like the sound of that.

And the sound of that was drifting out of Mrs O'Neill's open living-room window...

"Put it *down*! Oh dear, oh dear, oh dear! This is *terrible*!"

Pulling my heavy school bag up onto my shoulders, I hurried across to see what terrible things were going on at my neighbour's house...

"So ... he ate the whole bag of toffees?" Mum asked.

Mum was on the phone – I'd called her at the rescue centre, as soon as I took the **DIB** out of Mrs O'Neill's house and brought him round to ours.

"He ate the *whole* bag." I nodded, though Mum couldn't see that. "AND he ate a fruit basket that Mrs O'Neill had made out of ice-lolly sticks AND her copy of the *Radio Times*."

"Oh, dear," sighed Mum.

"I know," I mumbled.

Mrs O'Neill hadn't taken to the **DIB** one little bit – in fact, Mrs O'Neill had *begged* me to take him away.

"So what's he doing now?" Mum asked.

"Nothing much," I told her, gazing down at him.

The **DIB** had his fat face in my lap. He was staring up at me with soppy (crossed) brown eyes. His tail was **thudda-dudda-dudda**-ing on the kitchen floor.

He was making a funny hiccupping breathing sound.

I think he was trying to pant, but couldn't because his teeth were still welded together with toffee.

"I wonder why he acted so badly?" said Mum.

"I think it's 'cause the first thing Mrs O'Neill did was take his blankie and put it in the bin."

Mum just sighed again, I was sure, but I couldn't quite hear that because of all the tail **thudda-dudda-dudda**-ing going on.

And that wasn't the *only* noise; Kenneth had curled himself up *right* next to the **DIB** and started *purring*!

"Is he behaving himself now? He's not upsetting the dogs or Smudge, is he?" Mum asked (which was easier to hear than sighing).

"He's fine," I told her, scratching the top of the **DIB**'s ugly head. "They're all fine."

Smudge hadn't batted a catty eyelid when he walked up to her on the sofa and gave her a sniff. Speaking of sniffs, George and the **DIB** had sniffed each other's bum hello, and made friends straight away. And Kenneth seemed purrily happy to have him around.

"Well, if he's behaving himself at the moment, then we might as well let him stay the night. I'll take him back to the rescue centre tomorrow, and then see if that place is still free at the special long-term kennels."

The kennels where dogs would never know the feeling of carpet under their paws.

The kennels where dogs would never amble under the kitchen table to be fed tit-bits when parents (hopefully) weren't looking.

The kennels where dogs could never sneak up on your bed and go to sleep on your duvet, with their snores vibrating on your knees…

The **DIB** suddenly started to make that cute, *hurra-hurra-hurrrumph* humming noise and he was *drooling* onto my jeans with happiness.

This dog can't go to the special kennels! I

found myself thinking, in a sudden panic.
He's got to stay here!

"Mum!"

A pair of loving, dopey eyes were fixed on mine.

"What?"

"You know how you forgot my birthday last week?"

"Oh, Indie – I felt terrible about that, you know that!" Mum apologised. "I only forgot because I was worried about the hedgehogs, and I promise I'll never do it again!"

"But you *can*! You can forget *all* my birthdays from now on, Mum! I just want one present now, and I don't EVER want another one!"

There was just a second's pause from Mum, and I suddenly wondered if she was panicking that I was about to ask for her and Dad to get back together or something just as impossible.

"What is it, Indie?"

"I want the **DIB**! I mean, I want the **DIB** to come and live with us and Caitlin and George and Kenneth and Smudge and the fish!"

"Oh! Is that all? Oh, OK! Fine! Why not?"

Mum sounded so enthusiastic that I

KNEW she was well relieved that I didn't want her and Dad to get back together again.

Thudda-dudda-dudda…!

And I couldn't believe I was so mad about a darling, dumb dog that looked like a cross between a pot-bellied pig and a bin bag.

"Hear that? You're going to *live* with us!!" I smiled at the **DIB**, ruffling his furry head.

The **DIB** tried to bark, but his jaws were still stuck together with toffee.

"Poo … what's smelling in here?" asked Caitlin, ambling into the kitchen for a cup of tea.

OK, the **DIB** could stay, but that blankie had GOT to go…

13

♥

Hugs, happiness and drool...

It was Saturday morning and Soph and Fee had come round to mine to watch TV, eat crisps and pat my pets.

Ding dong!!!

Smudge had mistaken my lap for a very comfy bed, and when the doorbell rang she wasn't too thrilled at being poured onto the sofa, next to Soph, so I could go to answer it.

"Mee-hooooow! Mee-hooooow....!"

"Shush, Kenneth!" I heard Fee try to

calm him down, as I struggled to get to the front door past a bouncing George.

"Look! You're in the local paper!" said Dylan, from halfway down the path.

I felt a fluttering in my tummy, like a whole bunch of butterflies was as excited as I was.

"Come in!" I told Dylan, hurriedly.

Dylan looked at me blankly, as if I'd just asked him to take all his clothes off and dance around the garden.

I didn't have time for this; so I just left

the door ajar and hurried back through to
the kitchen, where I knew a lumpy black
blob would be cowering behind the bin.

Both Soph and Fee were trying to coax
him out with cooing and some crisps, but
with no luck.

"Is that Dibbles?" asked Dylan, finally
following me in and ignor-
ing my two best mates.
(He'd only met them a
couple of times before,
when we'd bumped
into him in town.)

"Yep, that's him," I
nodded, though all you
could see were two
worried brown eyes
peering over the bin.

I pulled a packet of toffees out of my

pocket and waved them at Dibbles – it seemed to do the trick and he began slinking towards me.

"What's wrong with him?"

"He doesn't like *doinggg*-ing sounds," I explained, as I made a big fuss of the most scaredy-cat dog in the world. "But Mum says we've got to  get him used it, and we can help by reassuring him if he's frightened of a noise."

It had been a couple of days now, and we'd realized that Dibbles ('cause that's his new name; his PROPER name) had a real phobia of the theme tune to the news on telly, and the sound of the toilet being flushed, as *well* as the doorbell. *All* of them got him scurrying behind the kitchen bin.

But with lots of hugs, he was already getting better. At least he'd stopped trying to clamber *into* the kitchen bin to hide any more…

"Hey, Dibbles…! Don't be scared!" murmured Dylan, crouching down beside me, Soph and Fee on the floor.

"So, let's see the paper, then!" I said, now that Dylan was doing the coaxing and patting for me.

Grabbing it from him, I sat cross-legged, with Soph and Fee gazing over my shoulders.

"Wow!" said Soph.

"It's on page two," said Dylan, so busy scratching Dibbles' head that he didn't notice we were already at page two.

"Wow!" said Fee.

Wow!, I said in my head, though I shouldn't have been so surprised – a photographer and journalist from the paper had come round to interview me yesterday after school. They said they were going to do a cute story about me adopting the un-adoptable dog from the shelter.

But the reason I was thinking *'Wow'* wasn't anything to do with the picture of me cuddling Dibbles (with his brand new, un-smelly, satin-edged blankie) … it was the headline.

INDIE HAS A TALENT FOR DOING GOOD!

Fee read aloud.

"Why have you gone all pink, Indie?" Dylan blinked my way. I ignored my step-brother and thought about the headline about me-having-a-talent-for-doing-good again.

Me!

Little old me! Little old pink-cheeked, embarrassed-by-that-compliment *me*!

I had a talent for doing good!

And you know something? It was true! Maybe I'd goofed up on stuff along the way, but in the last couple of weeks, I'd made *lots* of good stuff happen, whether I meant it to or not.

You want a list? OK, well…

1) I got **LOTS** of animals new homes at the shelter 'cause of writing CVs for them.

2) I cheered my dad up when he was feeling down, by (accidentally) making him laugh.

3) I started **everyone** using the (new, glass-fronted) noticeboard at school.

4) I made Mrs O'Neill realize that maybe she did need a pet for company, only not a toffee-eating one (Mum took her to the rescue centre this morning to choose a budgie).

AND BEST OF ALL,

5) I got Dibbles a new home - with us...

"I can put that down on my CV for Miss Levy now!" I said excitedly, pointing to the headline.

"Right, so you're good at doing good," nodded Fee. "But what *else* are you going to put down, Indie – you have to have three things, don't you?"

So I did…

"*I* know!" shouted Soph, making Dibbles almost start slinking for the bin again. "You're good at being patient 'cause Dibbles keeps eating all your stuff, but you haven't got cross with him once!"

"OK … if I write down that I'm good at being good AND good at being patient, then that still means I need to find *one* more talent…" I frowned.

"Hey, LOOK," muttered Fee, elbowing me.

I did what I was told and looked up, to see Dibbles smothering Dylan with licks.

"Uh-huh. So?"

"So, Dylan hasn't turned into a swollen, red puffball yet, has he?" Fee pointed out.

"So you're good at curing allergies!"

I was so pleased, I wanted to hug someone, so I hugged Dibbles, who was tail-
thumpingly happy to be hugged.

Still, just to be on the safe side, we made
Dylan spend the next half hour cuddling
George, shaking paws with Kenneth, let-
ting Smudge use him as a cushion and
wiggling his hands in the fishtank.

He didn't start sneezing or swelling or anything.

And that's when we realized that my step-mum Fiona (nice as she was) was maybe kind of slightly *paranoid*, and that Dylan WASN'T allergic to animals in the first place.

Dylan was very happy not to be a swollen, red, allergic puffball.

And I was very happy to find that my talent was being good at stuff.

"*Achoooo!*" sneezed Dylan suddenly, as Dibbles licked his face.

OK – so maybe Dylan was just a *bit* allergic-ish.

"Hey, Indie – *achooo!* – aren't those bite marks in the bottom of Caitlin's didgeridoo?" he asked.

Urgh ... maybe I should've stopped

Dibbles from chewing on that earlier.

Maybe I wasn't such a good person after all.

Maybe I was just good-*ish*.

And good-*ish* –

"*Achoooo!*"

– was all right –

thudda-dudda-dudda

– by me!

(PS Anyone got any ideas how I can stop Dibbles drooling on my jeans…?)